P9-CAN-985

BEAR, WOLF AND MOUSE

A Follett Beginning-To-Read Book
Level Three

BEAR, WOLF AND MOUSE

Jan Wahl

Illustrated by Kinuko Craft

FOLLETT PUBLISHING COMPANY
CHICAGO

For my Weronika

Text copyright © 1975 by Jan Wahl. Illustrations copyright © 1975 by Follett Publishing Company, a division of Follett Corporation. All rights reserved. No part of this book may be reproduced in any form without written permission from the publisher. Manufactured in the United States of America.

ISBN 0-695-30516-6 Paper Binding
ISBN 0-695-40516-0 Titan Binding

Library of Congress Catalog Card Number: 74-83610

Fourth Printing

Once beside a big forest there lived a Bear. He thought he was very handsome.

He always stopped and looked whenever he passed a mirror.

Those beautiful ears! That long fur! Those wonderful brown eyes!

But really he looked like any other bear.

Every night he asked his friends Wolf and Mouse
for supper.

He liked to hear what a great cook he was. And
most of all he liked to hear how handsome he was.

"How do I look tonight?" he would ask.

"You look grand!" Wolf would say.

"That's right!" Mouse would say.

Wolf and Mouse would laugh about it when Bear
left the room.

But Bear was happy, and Wolf and Mouse got a free supper.

One night Wolf and Mouse came as always.

"Guess what's tonight?" asked Bear.

"Peanut pancakes!" said Mouse.

"Popcorn pie?" asked Wolf.

"No! FLAMING GREEN-APPLE STEW!" said Bear. It was one of his great dishes.

Bear brought out the stew. But! He left the kettle on too long. The supper was terrible.

Wolf and Mouse headed for the door.

"What's wrong?" asked Bear. "Nobody said how handsome I am."

"You're not!" snapped Wolf.

"You've got dirt all over your fur!" added Mouse.

"Stay and have a pot of honey," said Bear. "I'm sorry about the stew!"

Angry Wolf and hungry Mouse ran out the door saying they would not come back.

The next day Bear went into the forest.

He wanted someone to say how handsome he was!

He came to a little house. A lady was shelling peas.

As soon as the lady saw him, she ran out the back door.

"Oh," said Bear. "I must look terrible!"

He sat down and started shelling peas for the lady to show he was a good bear.

Just then the husband came home.

"What are you doing?" shouted the man. "UGLY BEAST! You ate my wife!"

The man lifted a big broom. He started to bop Bear.

But Bear knew he had not eaten the lady. He was thinking of the words UGLY BEAST!

He threw the peas in the man's face and ran out.

Bear ran and ran. He wanted someone to tell him he was HANDSOME.

He came to a deep, blue pool and looked in. Yes—he seemed as handsome as ever!

Then the soft bank broke. Bear fell in.

His fur was wet and sticky when he climbed out. An old Raccoon started laughing.

"O.K.! What's so funny?" asked Bear. He had a frog on his head.

"You are," said Raccoon. "Look at yourself!"

"I just did!" said Bear.

He looked again. He could see he was wild and wet and funny.

"I thought I was BEAUTIFUL!" said Bear.

"Handsome is . . . as handsome does!" said Raccoon.

Bear lay down to dry off.

He wished he could cook again for Wolf and Mouse. He thought up a wonderful supper for them.

After supper, Wolf and Mouse might say, "What a HANDSOME Bear!"

The sun went down. The forest was pink and dark purple.

Bear did a sad little dance. A butterfly sat on his nose.

He went home. He was not sure if he was handsome.

"Handsome is," said Bear, "as handsome does!"

He cleaned his pots. He made a fire. He got out some very green apples.

Bear whistled.

HE'D MAKE THE BEST SUPPER IN THE WORLD!

Now, hungry Wolf was looking for supper. When night came, he went to sleep without food. He howled at the moon.

He lay there. He remembered the food cooked by Bear. Oh!

"Those were the best suppers of my life!"

The next day Wolf came to a town. A big party was going on—with a lot of food and drink.

He crawled under the table.

"YOW! A WOLF!"

Everything was thrown at him. Sticks! Chairs! Plates! They hurt!

Wolf ran back to the forest.

Little Mouse was also hungry. He was thin and cold.

He came to a row of cabbages. At last!

He started to eat. Mouse found the cabbages were bad.

He remembered how Bear would cook HIS cabbages! These were terrible.

Mouse hurried along. He ran till he heard a pack of wild dogs.

The dogs were chasing a squirrel. Poor Mouse thought they were chasing HIM!

He rolled back into the forest like a brown and gray ball.

Mouse rolled right into Wolf! Both said, "Well—here we are!"

They thought about friend Bear. It was supper time. It was getting dark.

They tried eating leaves. That really didn't help.
"Remember Bear's wonderful stew?" Wolf asked.
"DO I?" cried Mouse. "I can still smell it in the air!"
"Funny. So do I," said Wolf.

So they followed their noses. The noses hurried to
Bear's house.

A great smell took them to the window.

Bear tasted the hot, new stew. He set only one
plate. Then he sat.

But Bear didn't eat. Tears fell down his nose into
the plate!

"Oh, Wolf!" cried Bear. "Oh, Mouse! Friends! How I hate to eat without you! Where ARE you?"

"Here we are!" said the two together. Mouse and Wolf ran inside the house.

"We came to keep you company!"

Was there ever a happier spot than Bear's house?

Bear set two more plates. He dished up the stew.

Wolf and Mouse jumped to the table. They were VERY hungry.

But first the two sang together: "Best of all bears!" His ears stood up when he heard.

"You are The Most Beautiful Cook In The World!"

"What was that?" asked Bear, paws trembling.

"YOU ARE THE MOST BEAUTIFUL—
EXCITING—GOOD-LOOKING COOK IN THE
WHOLE WORLD!"

Wolf and Mouse shouted it with much feeling.

To show it was true, they ate every bite of stew that night.

And every night after!

Uses of This Book: Reading for fun. This easy-to-read story of three delightful animal characters is sure to excite the rich imaginations of children.

Word List

All of the 311 words used in *Bear, Wolf and Mouse* are listed. Regular possessives and contractions ('s, n't, 'd), regular verb forms (-s, -ed, -ing), and plurals of words already on the list are not listed separately, but the endings are given in parentheses after the word.

5 once
beside
a
big
forest
there
live(d)
Bear(s, 's)
he('d)
thought
was
very
handsome
always
stopped
and
look(ed, ing)
whenever
pass(ed)
mirror
those
beautiful
ears
that('s)

long
fur
wonderful
brown
eyes
but
really
like(d)
any
other
6 every
night
ask(ed)
his
friend(s)
Wolf
Mouse
for
supper(s)
to
hear(d)
what('s)
great
cook(ed)

most
of
all
how
do(ing)
I
tonight
would
you
grand
say(ing)
right
laugh(ing)
about
it
when
left
the
room
7 happy
got
free
one
came

as
guess
peanut
pancake(s)
said
popcorn
pie
no
flaming
green
apple(s)
stew
dish(es, ed)
8 brought
out
kettle
on
too
terrible
head(ed)
door
wrong
nobody
am

28

you're
not
snapped
you've
dirt
over
your
add(ed)
9 stay
have
pot(s)
honey
I'm
sorry
angry
hungry
ran
they
come
back
next
day
went
into
want(ed)
someone
little
house
lady
shell(ing)

pea(s)
10 soon
saw
him
she
oh
must
sat
down
start(ed)
show
good
just
then
husband
home
11 are
shout(ed)
man('s)
ugly
beast
ate
my
wife
lift(ed)
broom
bop
knew
had
eaten

think(ing)
word(s)
threw
in
face
12 tell
deep
blue
pool
yes
seem(ed)
ever
soft
bank
broke
fell
13 wet
sticky
climb(ed)
an
old
Raccoon
O.K.
so
funny
frog
at
yourself
did(n't)
14 again

could
see
wild
is
does
lay
dry
off
wish(ed)
up
them
15 after
might
sun
pink
dark
purple
sad
dance
butterfly
nose(s)
sure
if
16 clean(ed)
made
fire
some
whistled
make
best

world

17 now

sleep

without

food

howl(ed)

moon

remember(ed)

by

were

life

18 town

party

go(ing)

with

lot

drink

crawl(ed)

under

table

yow

everything

thrown

stick(s)

chair(s)

plate(s)

hurt

19 also

thin

cold

row

cabbage(s)

last

eat(ing)

found

bad

these

20 hurried

along

till

pack

dog(s)

chasing

squirrel

poor

roll(ed)

gray

ball

21 both

well

here

we

time

getting

22 tried

leaves

help

cried

can

still

smell

air

23 follow(ed)

their

took

window

taste(d)

hot

new

set

only

tear(s)

24 hate

where

two

together

inside

keep

company

happier

spot

than

25 more

jump(ed)

first

sang

stood

26 paws

trembling

exciting

whole

much

feeling

27 true

bite

ABOUT THE AUTHOR:

Jan Wahl left his native Ohio to study folk literature and film at the University of Copenhagen. Since 1962 he has been writing exclusively for children. He has dozens of books in print, including *The Muffletump Storybook*, *The Muffletumps' Christmas Party*, and *Five in the Forest* for Follett. Among his numerous awards is a First Prize presented by a jury of children at the Bologna Book Fair. *Bear, Wolf and Mouse* is Mr. Wahl's first book in the Beginning-To-Read series.